The Snow Child

A Viking Easy-to-Read Classic

by Harriet Ziefert
illustrated by Julia Zanes

VIKING

VIKING
Published by the Penguin Group
Penguin Putnam Books for Young Readers,
345 Hudson Street, New York, New York 10014, U.S.A.
Penguin Books Ltd, 27 Wrights Lane, London W8 5TZ, England
Penguin Books Australia Ltd, Ringwood, Victoria, Australia
Penguin Books Canada Ltd, 10 Alcorn Avenue, Toronto, Ontario, Canada M4V 3B2
Penguin Books (N.Z.) Ltd, 182-190 Wairau Road, Auckland 10, New Zealand

Penguin Books Ltd, Registered Offices: Harmondsworth, Middlesex, England

First published in 2000 by Viking and Puffin Books,
divisions of Penguin Putnam Books for Young Readers.

3 5 7 9 10 8 6 4 2

LIBRARY OF CONGRESS CATALOGING-IN-PUBLICATION DATA
Ziefert, Harriet.
The snow child / by Harriet Ziefert ; illustrated by Julia Zanes.
p. cm.
Summary: An elderly couple who long for a child build a snow
child which comes to life and makes them very happy — until the
coming of spring when the days become too warm for her to stay.
ISBN 0-670-88748-X (hardcover) — ISBN 0-14-130577-0 (pbk.)
[1. Folklore—Russia.] I. Zanes, Julia, ill. II. Title.
PZ8.1.Z55 Sn 2000
398.2'0947'01— dc21
00-008767

Viking® and Easy-to-Read® are registered trademarks of Penguin Putnam Inc.

Printed in Hong Kong
Set in Bookman

Reading Level: 1.7

The Snow Child

An old man and his wife
lived together in a little old house.
They loved each other,
but they were not happy.
They wanted a child.

They wanted a little boy
or a little girl very much.

They watched the boys and girls make a big snowman. The man said to his wife, "Let's go outside and make a snow child." "That would make me happy," said his wife.

They made a body.

They made a head.

They added eyes,
and a nose,
then a mouth.

"She needs hair,"
said the old man.

"And a dress," said
the old lady.

"She's pretty," said the old man.
"Very pretty."
"Yes," said the old lady.
And she kissed the snow child.
The snow child came to life!
She moved her head,
then her arms, then her legs.
The little girl said,
"I am a child of the snow.
I come from the cold.
I am warmed by your kiss."

They carried the little girl
into their house.

The old woman sang
and the snow child danced.

"Here is your bed,"
said the old woman.
"It's time to go to sleep."

But the snow child said,
"No. I cannot sleep inside.
I must always sleep outside."

And out she ran!

She slept outside
on a bed of snow.
And every night the old
man and the old woman
made sure she was safe.

The snow child played with
the boys and girls next door.

They made many things
out of snow.

In spring, the snow began to melt.
Everyone was happy.
But not the snow child.

"What's wrong?"
asked the old woman.

"Are you sick?"
asked the old man.

"Nothing is wrong,"
said the snow child.

But she grew sadder
and sadder every day.

One morning the snow child
said, "I must go."
"Why?" cried the old woman.
"Don't go!   Please!"
"I am a child of the snow.
I must go where it is cold."
And the snow child ran away.

The old man and
the old woman cried.
They thought they would
never be happy again.

But when snow came again,
they looked out the window.
And who was there?

The snow child!

"I am a child of the snow.
I come back when it is cold."